牛
Ox

虎
Tiger

兔
Rabbit

鼠
Rat

龍
Dragon

豬
Plg

蛇
Snake

For nearly 5,000 years, the Chinese culture
has organized time in cycles of twelve years.
This Eastern calendar is based upon the movement
of the moon (as compared to the Western which
follows the sun) and is symbolized by the zodiac circle.
An animal that has unique qualities represents each year.
Therefore, if you are born in a particular year,
then you share the personality of that animal.
Now people worldwide celebrate this
two-week long festival in the early spring and enjoy
the start of another Chinese New Year.

狗
Dog

馬
Horse

雞
Rooster

猴
Monkey

羊
Sheep

To Uncle Hank whose smile, pawshake, and wit
established many a friendship.
— O.C.

To Alexandra, the utmost authority on all things cute.
Without your support and incredible patience, this would
not have been possible. I love you.

And to my parents whose love, encouragement, and
life–long sacrifices have allowed me to follow my dreams.
Thank you so very much. You are the best!
— J.R.

immedium

Immedium, Inc.   P.O. Box 31846   San Francisco, CA 94131
www.immedium.com

Text Copyright ©2010 Oliver Chin
Illustrations Copyright ©2010 Justin Roth

First hardcover edition published 2010.

Edited by Don Menn
Book design by Elaine Chu
Calligraphy by Lucy Chu

Printed in Singapore
10 9 8 7 6 5 4 3 2 1

Chin, Oliver Clyde, 1969-
  The year of the tiger : tales from the Chinese zodiac / by Oliver Chin ;
illustrated by Justin Roth. -- 1st hardcover ed.
      p. cm.
  Summary: The adventures and misadventures of Teddy the tiger cub as he learns that "good manners
make good neighbors." Lists the birth years and characteristics of individuals born in the Chinese Year of
the Tiger.
  ISBN-10: 1-59702-020-6 (hardcover)
  [1. Tiger--Fiction. 2. Animals--Infancy--Fiction. 3. Astrology, Chinese--Fiction] I. Roth, Justin, , ill. II. Title.
  PZ7.C44235Yer 2010
  [E]--dc22

2009012497
ISBN: 1-59702-020-6
ISBN 13: 978-159702-020-6

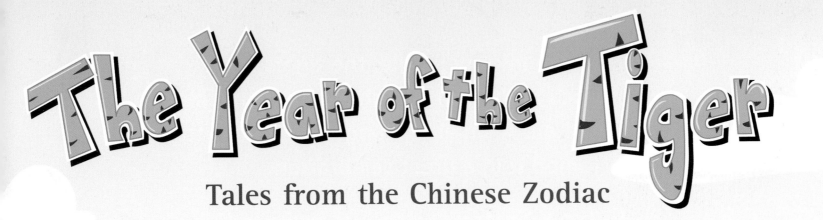

The Year of the Tiger

Tales from the Chinese Zodiac

Written by Oliver Chin
Illustrated by Justin Roth

immedium
Immedium, Inc.
San Francisco

In the mighty jungle, the tigers slept each night. But tonight excitement filled the air. A small cry rang out. Then catcalls joined it in a great celebration.

The King and Queen just had a baby!

As the morning sunshine warmed the royal den, the cub yawned loudly, **"Roar!"**

The Queen whispered, "Hush, my darling."

Cuddling his newborn, the King chuckled, "Theodore, you are a feisty chap."

Soon this fur ball roamed the forest like it was his own backyard. His parents marveled at his curiosity. Teddy meowed,
"I'm becoming a big cat!"

The Queen laughed, "Someday you'll be king of the jungle."

Later she advised, "Son, a wise ruler
starts out as a careful prince."

The King added, "We've heard of
dangerous animals called 'humans.'
Their houses and roads invade our land,
so stay away from them."

CHOP!

But this warning tickled the kitten's interest.
"I want to see these beasts for myself,"
gushed Teddy. He learned that people lived on
the edge of the forest. So one evening,
he set out alone in that direction.

After a while he came to a ridge. In the glen below were thatched roofs, dirt paths, and a person sitting in a field!

To get a better look, Teddy sneaked down the hill and his striped coat blended into the tall reeds.

The clearing of short grass felt strange under his feet. Distracted by a rat, he gleefully pounced after it and snarled, **"Roar!"**

However, he startled the nearby ox and horse, which frantically galloped off.

In the moonlight, the girl saw Teddy and froze in surprise. Su screamed, "Tiger! Tiger!"

The cat scampered into the trees. Racing back to the palace, he thought, "That creature was quite a fright."

Meanwhile, the villagers searched for the intruder. But they found neither hide nor hair of Teddy.

"Su, don't cry 'tiger' when there isn't one!" chided her father, Ba-Ba.

At home, Teddy didn't tell his parents about his close encounter. But he couldn't stop thinking about the girl.

So early one morning, he returned to town and spotted the barn where Su fed the livestock.

Inside, Su served breakfast to the sheep and pig. Not wanting to scare anyone, Teddy said, **"Good morning."**

Sharp teeth filled the tiger's smile.

The animals squealed, "Run for your lives!"

Teddy sprang backwards into a
haystack. Su laughed since she,
too, had thought of the tiger.

"You must be thirsty,"
she said and poured
a bowl of milk.
"Here kitty, kitty."

BURP!

Intrigued, Teddy took
a sip. Licking the bowl
clean, the tiger purred,
"I'm Teddy."

Rubbing her nose to his, she replied, "I'm Su. Do you want to play?"

Suddenly, Su's mother opened the door. Teddy jumped outside to the woods beyond.

Staring at the orange blur across her field, Ma-Ma cried, "It's the tiger!"

Ba-Ba told Su to stay inside with the dog,
"Remember, it's better to be safe than sorry!"
Then he and Ma-Ma left to warn their neighbors.

Back in the jungle, the King scowled, "Teddy, we know where you've been. We told you to avoid those people."

The Queen sighed, "The outsiders have gotten too close. Now we must find a new home."

Obediently packing his belongings, Teddy wondered, **"Why are we afraid of them when they are scared of me?"**

But he still wanted to see Su one last time, so he slipped away to the girl's house.

As the tiger crept closer,
the watchdog growled,
"Who goes there?"

Trying to be friendly,
Teddy offered a pawshake,
"Hello, there."

Yet sharp claws popped out, and
the terrified pooch scampered off.

Opening the door, Su asked, "Teddy, why are you here?"

He blushed, **"My family is moving, so I came to say goodbye."**

Su giggled, "Oh silly, you didn't have to." But a loud noise interrupted them.

The dog returned with Su's parents, who yelled,
"There's the man-eater! Get him!"

The villagers gave chase, and Teddy fled again.
But unexpectedly, Su followed her new friend
into the wild.

In the bush, the pair dashed ahead, and gradually squawks of birds replaced the roar of the crowd.

Su had never ventured beyond her farm before. With Teddy as her guide, she marveled at wondrous sights.

Miles away, the Queen wondered, "Where's Teddy?" The King got wind that humans had entered the jungle.

Immediately they dropped everything and raced to find their son.

On one end of the forest, Ma-Ma and Ba-Ba tracked Su's footsteps.

On the other, the King and Queen caught Teddy's scent.

Unaware of the two hunting parties, the girl and tiger innocently hiked along.

The youngsters wandered
toward a cliff, where Teddy showed
Su the spectacular waterfalls.

As she admired the lovely
view, he saw his bright stripes,
sharp teeth, and claws
in a reflecting pool.

Teddy always considered himself like everyone else. Now why did people dislike him for being different? Su didn't mind at all.

While he was lost in thought, Su accidentally stepped on a snake, sleeping in the grass!

!

SQUISH

The serpent gave a loud "Hiss!"

Su slipped on a stone. Tipping backwards over the ledge, she cried, "Help!"

Shaken from his daydream, Teddy turned in disbelief. What could he do?

Instinctively the cat leapt forward to save Su.
Bounding into the chasm below,
Teddy shouted,

"Roar!"

Slowly opening her eyes, Su was surprised that she had stopped falling. Instead, she saw Teddy's toothy grin. His strong bite held onto her as his claws clutched the dangling branches of a tree.

With a mighty effort, the tiger dragged the girl up. They rested to catch their breath.

Then Su grabbed onto his tail, and Teddy led the way as they carefully climbed up.

Hearing their children's voices, the worried parents rushed to them.

Arriving at the same time, they saw Teddy pull Su back to safety. Confused, each group warily kept their distance.

The cat and girl knew what to do.
They held their parents' hands
and brought them together.

Ma-Ma and Ba-Ba smiled.
The King was puzzled.
"Dear, our little prince is
growing up indeed," laughed
the Queen.

Afterwards, each family invited the other over to play. Traveling between treetop and rooftop, the adults were amazed how well everybody got along. "Good manners make good neighbors," they all agreed.

Su and Teddy enjoyed swimming and singing.
They shared nature walks and bedtime stories.

And in the jungle, both man and beast would
recall that this was a terrific Year of the Tiger!

虎
Tiger
1914, 1926, 1938, 1950, 1962, 1974, 1986, 1998, 2010, 2022

People born in the Year of the Tiger are bold and proud. These warm souls are courageous and charismatic. But sometimes they reveal different stripes when they are rash and unpredictable. Though they may seem secretive and catty, tigers prove to be the fiercest of friends.